Henry Neville Maugham

The Husband of Poverty

Henry Neville Maugham

The Husband of Poverty

ISBN/EAN: 9783337334406

Printed in Europe, USA, Canada, Australia, Japan

Cover: Foto ©Andreas Hilbeck / pixelio.de

More available books at **www.hansebooks.com**

FRANCIS OF ASSISI.

The
Husband of Poverty.

A DRAMA OF THE LIFE OF
FRANCIS OF ASSISI.

By HENRY NEVILLE MAUGHAM.

> " Perch' io non procedar troppo chiuso,
>   Francesco e Poverta per questi amanti
>   Prendi oramai nel mio parlar diffuso."
>   DANTE.

BOSTON :
COPELAND & DAY, 69 CORNHILL.
1897.

THE PERSONS.

FRANCIS of Assisi.
PIETRO DI BERNARDONE, his Father.
BISHOP OF ASSISI.

ELIAS,
BERNARD,
JUNIPER,
LEO,
SYLVESTER,
GILES,
} Brothers of the first Order founded by Francis.

CONRAD,
NICHOLAS,
JOACHIM,
} Friends of Francis' youth.

Consuls, Magistrates of Assisi.
CECCO, a pipe-player.
A Peasant, a Soldier.

CLARE, as a young maiden, afterwards Superior of the second
    Order founded by Francis.
PICA, Mother to Francis.
HÉLEN, a Novice.
GIACOMA DE SETTESOLI, of the Lay Order founded by Francis.
A Poor Woman.

Brothers and Sisters of the Orders, ANGELO (second son to
    PIETRO), Citizens of Assisi, Children, attendant on CLARE,
    a Doctor, sons of GIACOMA and her retinue, sons of CECCO,
    Confessor to the Bishop of Assisi, Captain and Guard,
    Marauders, Foresters.

SCENE: Assisi and places near.

SYNOPSIS.

Act I. The marriage with Poverty.

Act II. Francis preaches to the birds.

Act III. Sister Clare.

Act IV. The bride of snow.

Act V. The final seals.

Illustrations.—St. FRANCIS, drawn by the author after Fra Angelico. VIEW OF ASSISI, from the "Collis Paradisi Amœnitas" (1704).

THE HUSBAND OF POVERTY.

ACT I.

The Piazza before the Cathedral. A tavern to the left, with tables set without ; to the right the Bishop's house, with his arms over the door. NICHOLAS *leaving the cathedral gives alms to a beggar, and bows to* JOACHIM *and* CONRAD, *who return the courtesy.*

NICHOLAS.

GOOD morrow, Joachim, and to your friend.
Surely we knew you, sir, before the wars ?

JOACHIM.

Surely we knew him, gentle Nicholas !

NICHOLAS.

Certes, 'tis Conrad ! Here's my hand and heart.

CONRAD.

And mine ; I well remember Nicholas.

NICHOLAS.

'Tis well that friends should meet in hostile times ;
Let's drink a cup to further amity.

JOACHIM.

We are delighted.

B

NICHOLAS.
Host, a flask of wine.

CONRAD.
How often, wandering, I've longed to drink
The mellow wine of Umbria's fertile plains!

JOACHIM.
There is no vintage of its worth abroad.

NICHOLAS.
That's true, but e'en our wine's a bitter draught,
When treachery has pressed with stealthy feet
The sicklied grape.   [*The* Host *brings wine.*
                    But here's a four years' growth
That sunned itself in an untainted air.
Here's love to friends and death to traitors' souls.
                              [*They drink.*

CONRAD.
It angers me to think I was away——

NICHOLAS.
Rejoice that you were so ; your noble heart
Had burst to see the town in its distress.
Myself, I took a wound, which painfully eased
The passion of my blood, and Joachim,
Taken in bonds to proud Perugia,
Was happier with true foes than faithless friends.

CONRAD.
The nobles of the town——

NICHOLAS.
                    Our noble rulers,
Who fought against us with our enemies,
And made their victory an easy thing.

CONRAD.

And how bears up the town in its disgrace?

NICHOLAS.

Sadly. The most considered citizens
Creep out abashed amid our humbled streets,
The crowd holds sullen silence, old wives weep,
Our maidens are less fair and stay at home,
The moonlit nights that erst were glad with song
And bands of lovers singing to their dears,
Are sad and voiceless; songs and love are dead;
And to our great distress, young Bernardone,
Our little king of laughter and good looks,
Who had the smartest dress and sleekest curls,
Who won more loves and made more riotry
Than any of us, though we plume ourselves
As not deficient in accomplishments,
Knew more of horseflesh, and could play a sword
Better than any these ignoble nobles,
He, our example, envy, and delight,
Has caught the general mildew and grown mean.

CONRAD.

What! Francis Bernardone?

NICHOLAS.
                        Even so.

JOACHIM.

What's more, he's caused his courage to be doubted.

CONRAD.

Francis a coward? But we loved him so!

NICHOLAS.

Here is the tale. It is not pleasant hearing.
Let's fill our glasses first. Here's to our loves——

No doubt you've won a many travelling.

> [CONRAD *shows a portrait.*

Ah! that's a handsome wench! Our little Conrad!
When we had peace and were released from bonds,
A company of gentlemen resolved
To take up arms with Gauthier de Brienne,
A cavalier who bore the Papal arms,
Among them Francis, who, in fine array,
His page's buckler set upon his arm,
Started with the applauded cavalcade,
Singing of chivalry, and to his father,
A fine old man who never spoiled his pranks,
Saying, " I'll win my knighthood in the wars ;
You'll be as proud as you've been good to me ; "
And the old man was all aglow with joy
To see his son among the crested knights,
And all admired to see their kind farewell.
Thus Francis rode away to win his spurs ;
But scarcely had he reached Spoleto's towers,
When, angered at the jests of worthier men,
Who had less brave array but stouter hearts,
Or for a touch of sickness, as some say,
Perhaps the sudden colic known as fear,
He leaves the troop—I'm telling you a fact—
And seeks in coward haste his safer home.

JOACHIM.
Remember he avers a vision seen.

CONRAD.
He had no pluck, I take it, for the war ;
He was a sad impostor.

NICHOLAS.
> Mark the sequel.
His father's justly angered, and he flies
For fear of whipping to protecting priests,
Makes loud profession of a penitent mind,

Pulling long faces, taking desolate paths,
Talking with beggars, kissing lepers' hands.

CONRAD.

Faugh! 'tis a filthy sight to see the fellow
Turning a saint for very cowardice.

JOACHIM.

The saints were often sinners in their youth.

NICHOLAS.

I love the saints who hallowed ancient days,
But they by heaven's will and their pure lives
Became the objects of our veneration.
Our warlike days have little need of saints ;
And if such wonders could be seen to-day,
Christ has the choice of many a goodly man.
The saints were true, and loved their natal towns,
And often brought the angels to their aid ;
The saints were sensible, and would observe
Love for their lowly kind progenitors;
The saints would help the clean and honest poor,
And not the lepers who show Heaven's wrath.
But what is this ?   The coward fool again !

Enter FRANCIS *in rags, followed by* Children.

CHILDREN.

Pazzo, pazzo !

NICHOLAS.

Watch him awhile : this was our Francis once.

FIRST CHILD.

Good-morrow, fool, may I hold your cloak for you ?

FRANCIS.

Poor child, you're thinly clad for such a season.

SECOND CHILD.

Give us a soldo for holy charity.

FRANCIS.

Here is my blessing, I have nothing else.

THIRD CHILD.

Will you sell us a drop of your sweat, Ser Francesco ?

FRANCIS.

All that I have is long-time sold to God.

FIRST CHILD.

Will you sing us a song then ?

CHILDREN.

Yes, a song from the fool !   Hush, hush !

FRANCIS.

I'll sing for ye, if ye will list to hear.

[*Sings.*] There was a knight of Bethlehem,
        Whose wealth was tears and sorrows ;
    His men-at-arms were little lambs,
        His trumpeters were sparrows ;
    His castle was a wooden cross,
        Whereon he hung so high ;
    His helmet was a crown of thorns
        Whose crest did touch the sky.

CHILDREN.

Pazzo pazzo ! Oh, what a fine song ! Well sung, fool.

FIRST CHILD.

Your song is most beautiful.   Here is your wreath.
                                    [*Throws mud on him.*

CONRAD.

How now, young knaves, ye do disturb the streets.

[*Cuffs them.*

JOACHIM.

Get hence.

FRANCIS.

I pray you suffer them awhile.

NICHOLAS.

We do remember you were once a friend.

[*Strikes a boy, who cries.*

FRANCIS.

Poor child! I pray you do not smite my friends.

NICHOLAS.

Get hence, or you'll have something fit for tears;

[*Exeunt* Children.

Stay here, I tell you, Francis.

FRANCIS.

I obey,

If thou wilt hit thine anger out on me.

CONRAD.

Blows you'll not have of us, but pity, yes.

FRANCIS.

I thank you, pity well befits my past.

NICHOLAS.

Ah! stay that whine and hearken to our love.
Once you were of us; never will you be
As then, but still you may redeem yourself.
Repent your sins, if you would be a priest,
But do the thing with righteous decency.
Here, take this wine, you tremble with the cold.

FRANCIS.

I thank you.

NICHOLAS.
What, he gives it to a beggar?

FRANCIS.
I am refreshed, my limbs were somewhat chilled.
[NICHOLAS *rises.*

CONRAD.
Patience!   Do you remember me?

FRANCIS.
I do.
And once I smote you, and I pray you now
To beat me heartily.   Here is a stick.
[*Taking the beggar's staff.*
Why do you weep?

CONRAD.
Poor friend!   I weep for you.

FRANCIS.
I thank you for those tears; I'll weep for you.

JOACHIM.
Indeed we waste our words.

FRANCIS.
Indeed you do.
You shall not take me back unto your prison:
The festering chains of richly wove attire,
The unsubstantial banquets of fat food,
The long dark hours of lust, the turning wheel
Of hate that breaks the bodies of our love.
I will no longer make my sorry jest,
Mocked by the tyrant prince Iniquity,
Nor will I dance before him in his halls.
I have undone the curse and broke my bonds.

The Children *return with a volley of stones and take
flight, while* CLARE *enters with an* Attendant.

CLARE.

Poor man! a stone has struck him and he bleeds.

FRANCIS.

How sweet the word of pity from a child!

NICHOLAS.

It is the Lady Clare, child of the Sciffi.

CONRAD.

She is a maid a man would fight to win.

CLARE.

Friend, take my handkerchief.   Dear governess,
Have we no alms to give him?

FRANCIS.

Come not near;
'Tis not for innocence to touch my hand.

JOACHIM.

He means no evil, but his mind's obscured.

CLARE.

His looks are gentle and his eyes are sad;
If he will come unto my father's house
He shall be cared for.   Come, my gentle nurse.
                              [*Exit with* Attendant.

NICHOLAS.

Poor Francis, you're not fit for holy life;
Even a simple girl can stir your blood.

FRANCIS.

And if my heart were full of noisome thoughts,
Were it not stronger reason for my lust
To seek the yoke of sternest discipline?

It matters little what you think of me,
For till my heart is innocent as that child's,
It will not be the heart that I must make it.
O childhood tenderly compassionate,
Could I but imitate thine instant love
That knows nor rank nor shame nor outward seeming,
That feigns not friendship nor dissembles hate,
But sweetly gives itself in charity!

JOACHIM.
He talks as if he were an old, old man.

FRANCIS.
I have lived a long, long life away from God.

Enter PICA.

PICA.
Francis, my son, Francis, my dearest child,
Your father knows your sojourn in the town,
And even now comes on with armèd men.
He says you stole some goods and took their price
For your own uses.   Fly without delay.

FRANCIS.
Dear, cherished mother, do not grieve for me,
For from the deep, dark dungeon where I lie
I see the light of my deliverance.

PICA.
Why didst thou take the money?   Well you know—
But fly, I hear them come.

FRANCIS.
                You bid me fly,
But, mother mine, this is my wedding day.

NICHOLAS.
And even to his mother insolent!

PICA.

Alas! It is too late.

Enter PIETRO, *with* ANGELO, Consuls, Captain *and the* Guard, Citizens.

PIETRO.
See how he stands,
The son of honourable citizens,
Who toiled with all the love that parents know
To make his place a fine and worthy one!
Long dangerous journeys did I undertake,
And long time was my Pica left alone,
For this our child, and often did we speak,
My wife and I, beside his little bed
In whispers of his future. See him smile.
I'm no choleric father, feared and shunned;
I nurtured him with grave, restrainèd love,
Forgave his follies and extravagance,
Perhaps was proud of them, as fathers are.
I would have had him carry on my business;
He wished to take up arms; I acquiesced,
And bought him an equipment for the wars.
You know how long he followed with the flag.

CITIZENS.
He is justly angry.—He ought to have been more severe.

PIETRO.
Hear me and judge me. Even cowardice
I could forgive, because he was my son:
But when he comes in shameful mockery,
Talks of his sins, and tries to play the saint,
Shunning our sights as though we were his lepers,
Reproves me for my pride, my avarice,
I who had only pinched to win him wealth,
And with his boasted vows of poverty
Steals from my goods and dissipates my store,

Casts to the winds the patience of long years,
Estranges his own mother from her spouse,—
That was the term to fatherly forbearance.

CITIZENS.

The trouble wouldn't have happened if Pietro hadn't
sent his son among gentlemen.—My sons don't give
me any trouble.

PIETRO.

A taste of jail will do the caitiff good.
Observe, I shame my name to win him back.
When he has cooled his heels in yonder prison,
I'll send him out into the world again.
Now, consuls, do your work.

FRANCIS.
                        One word, I pray.

PICA.

Francis, be silent to thy father's wrath.

FRANCIS.

Mother, be sure, if ever filial love
Was wanting in my heart, it is not now,
When I must go an orphan.   I have been
A thankless son, selfish, undutiful ;
He should not much miss me, who never made
Any return.   His anger is most just.
He saved and thought for me, and all I gave
Was black ingratitude and cowardice.

CITIZENS.

There, he confesses his fault.

FRANCIS.

Let me continue.   Thou, O father dear,
Wast ever worthy and most generous,
And yet the worst of fathers ; ofttimes love

Does grievous harm because it will not see
Its gifts are less of helps than hindrances.
Thy love paternal offers wealth and ease,
Consideration, honour and a home ;
Thou only askest for a little grandson
To sit upon thy knee, and then content
Thou wilt descend to take thy just repose.

PIETRO.
And why should not this be ?

FRANCIS.
      I do not know
Why Heaven parts us, why our private lives
Should be dissevered, why I should stand thus,
A misery to myself and scorn to others ;
Why these things are, I do not understand,
Only I know those things will never be.

CONSUL.
Francis, consider well thy father's love.

FRANCIS.
I have considered it and find it wanting.

CITIZENS.
Shame on you, Francis.—He goes too far.—Who
would have thought him so cold in heart.—He de-
serves whipping.

CONSUL.
We make you prisoner, young Bernardone.

FRANCIS.
You cannot.

CONSUL.
    Cannot ! Captain, do your duty.

FRANCIS.

I plead the benefit of clergy.

PIETRO.
                    So!
You think the Bishop's eye will countenance
Your heartlessness.

CONSUL.
                    How do you ground your plea?

FRANCIS.

I am a clerk.

CONSUL.
                    (Perhaps that's fortunate.
These private quarrels only make us foes.)
My man, go in, present my humble duty,
And ask his lordship if he can receive me.
                    [*Exit one of the* Guard.

PIETRO.

Once it was thought a son would tell his father
When he a clerk became, but then that was
In the old days long past when we were young.

CAPTAIN.

You press too far.   Get back.   The Bishop comes.

Enter the BISHOP *with his* Confessor.

THE BISHOP.

Peace be with you, my friends ; what have we now?

CONSUL.

Pietro Bernardone has accused
His son Francesco of a certain theft.
The accused has pleaded benefit of clergy :
If your kind lordship thinks the plea is good,
We only wish to put him in your hands.

THE BISHOP.

'Tis of our knowledge that he is a clerk.

CONSUL.

Then is our office ended, good my lord.

THE BISHOP.

Do you uphold your accusation, sir?
You look disturbed, and we would counsel you
To wait on your decision till the morrow;
Meanwhile your son shall be in our safe hands.

PIETRO, *kneeling before the* BISHOP *with* PICA.

My lord bishop, I accuse not my son of thieving
aught from me, save himself. I wish to have him
back to my love; your lordship sees he is in piteous
plight. Bid him, we pray you, come back to us.
We are good simple folk, Pica and I; God gave
us a son, shall that son take God's gift from us?
We are old folk, we have worked late and risen early
for our children's good; they should not leave us in
our old age. When your lordship took holy orders,
we are sure you did not disdain your parents; he
hates us, and takes our savings to give to his beggar
companions. Your lordship knows we have done
acts of charity; we gave fifty crowns to the poor
when your lordship came to the see, and ten yearly
to the parish church, latterly increased to fifteen,
and much alms to our poorer neighbours. Francis
is very young, my lord; I have perhaps been hard
on him. If you will give him a good counsel, he will
return and be a good lad. See you, he weeps.

CITIZENS.

Pietro has been a good father.—We all swear to that,
my lord.—Francis will be a good son again.—Let his
lordship speak.

The Bishop.

Your son came lately to us to request
Our counsel in this matter, and with tears
Lamented of his life and of the hurt
His father's love would take of his withdrawal
Into the straighter road.   We feel your grief.
You are not the first father who has grieved
Because a son has left his earthly home
To seek a heavenly.   There we weep with you.
But we must needs rejoice to find a lamb
Come young into the fold, and with your tears
Our gladness must conflict.   Come hither, Francis.
The day is come for thee to justify
The vows of a conversion which began
In some extravagance.   In your brief years
You have done much of evil, little good,
And it was time that you grew wise to see
The errors of your ways.   We had preferred
More modest change of mind, but as it seems
Your heart requires this mode of penitence,
We do not blame it, only we require
To be assured of its continuing.
Two paths are set before thee for thy choice,
And each is good, though one is holier ;
Be wise to choose, that when the choice is made,
It may be final, not to be revoked ;
And that thy steady footsteps still may walk
The road thou hast determined on to-day.

Francis.

This is a great event for me,
A serious and a solemn occasion ;
It is my bridal day.
There is my mother who bore me,
There the font of my baptism,
These my fellow-citizens,
You, my lord, the priest,
This is my wedding garment.

CITIZENS.

His speech is strange.—Has he offended Heaven ?
—He is mad.

FRANCIS.

I strangely won the maiden of my choice.
You all remember how I proved a coward ;
'Twas when I went to fight
With Gauthier de Brienne.
All that day I sang of feats of arms ;
When the night came I could not sleep
For thinking of this Gauthier de Brienne,
Hoping that I should die for him
In some terrific fight.
As I fought and fell for him,
Smiling with dying lips to have his praise,
Another knight came to me :
In the dim early hours
I saw him stand beside my bed.
About his gentle face a coif de mailles
Such as no earthly armourer
Has for mightiest prince devised !
His hauberk was a beauteous marvel,
But not brighter anywise
Than his stockings of mail and golden spurs.
Over all
A surcoat of white sarcenet,
Whereon a cross did shine !
He bore a fair cross-hilted sword,
A blazoned shield hung on his back :
Thus was my knight arrayed.

CITIZENS.

Who was the knight came to him ?—Let him
continue.

FRANCIS.

I felt this knight did love me well, and said,
" What can I do for thee ? "
He looked intent into my eyes and said,

D

"Thou must be of my troop."
"Kind knight," I said, "I serve
With Gauthier de Brienne ;
If I desert this gallant cause
A coward I shall prove."
The knight looked again on me,
"Then be my coward," he replied.
He came and sat upon the bed,
But I still obstinate,
"With my Gauthier de Brienne
A pair of spurs I'll win."
"Of me thou shalt have scorn
As thy grave sins well deserve,
Hunger and blows and hate,
The meanest place of all."
The knight so fairly said this word,
That I replied, "I almost find it wise
To serve with thee."
He leant on me and sighed.
I took his hand to comfort him,
And saw a wound thereon as of a nail.

> *[The people cross themselves.*

I knelt to him
And said, "O knight, thy coward I will be!"
Hearken awhile.
The knight then told me of his wars,
Told me of his ancestral home,
Showed me his shield,
Charged with the emblems of the passion,
And promised me not spurs, but wings,
If well I fought ;
And further promised me a bride—
Her name is Poverty.
And now my bridal day is come ;
Here are my parents, my friends ;
The children have thrown flowers ;
Hark to the wedding bells!

> *[The bells ring from the tower.*

CITIZENS.

Didn't think 'a could talk like that.—A father
should not hamper a wise son.

THE BISHOP.

Thus you do choose to walk the straighter road.

FRANCIS.

And I am now husband to Poverty.

PIETRO.

Go then your way ; I have another son.
Come hither, Angelo ; forgive thy father
Who has preferred ingratitude to thee ;—
And that reminds me, I must have that straight.
Francis, my lord, I will not say my son,
I fear will seek to have his lawful share
Of my inheritance when I am gone,
And thus would cheat my son, my only son
Who's true to me ; if Francis is sincere,
Let him renounce his heirship unto me.

CITIZENS.

He won't give up his rights.—Not he !

THE BISHOP.

The father's plea is just.   What do you say ?

FRANCIS.

Before your lordship I renounce my share
In all the goods of Messer Bernardone,
Whom once I father called ; and for the earnest,
Here are the only things of his I have,
Useless cerements ; this last frail garment thin,
I ask to keep till I can get another.

> [*He throws off his clothes.*

PICA.

Poor child, he'll take his death.

FRANCIS.
Farewell, poor rags!
Henceforward I shall wear a brighter garment.

THE BISHOP.
I weep for joy to see thee do this thing ;
Come to my heart and let me shelter thee.

JUNIPER.
My lord, here's my cloak for him.   A mean one
enough, but willingly given.

FRANCIS.
I thank thee, friend.

CITIZENS.
Well done, cobbler.   Thou'lt be a saint next.

JUNIPER.
I'll break the head of any man as tries to fool me.

FRANCIS.
Tell me, what is thy name?

JUNIPER.
Juniper.

FRANCIS.
Who knows but I may need thee for a staff?
[*To a* Painter.] My friend, hast thou a brush of paint
to spare?
[*Paints a cross on the back of the tunic.*
I thank you.   My equipment is complete.
I will go forth with my wounded knight,
He has such sad eyes,
He died for me,
I am his coward.
Thus I go forth.
I shall come back

To announce his victories.
He takes the world captive ;
Surely this little town ;
The walls crumble before him ;
I see the streets filled with smiling prisoners,
Showering flowers and glad tears ;
These bring the city's allegiance,
Those pay tribute to the saints.
And there upon the mountain snows,
Our gentle conqueror
And peerless knight,
Christ our King.

I am the herald of the great King,
I am the herald of the great King,
I am the herald of the great King.

> [*Exit.* PIETRO *stoops down and takes away
> the clothes amid a silence.*

ACT II.

A terrace by the ruined Chapel of the Carceri. A shrine of the Madonna. A rude well, rocks, shrubs, and the springlit hillside. JUNIPER *alone.*

JUNIPER.

BROTHER Bernard to visit a sick woman, Elias to confer with the Bishop of Assisi, Sylvester to say the office of the Porziuncula, Brother Juniper to mend shoes and cook for the brethren. There's no disputing it, I have the humblest work to-day. Brother Juniper, pride is a sin. There can be pride in humility. I've caught you again in your wicked pride. Two paternosters and an ave for that. Insensate, shocking, satanic pride! I'll give you a gloria too.

Now, shall I cook first, or cobble first? Cobbling's my trade, cooking's my pleasure. Then let me do my work first, as it irks me. No, for then I shall be looking forward to my cooking. Then cook first. No, for the brothers would have cold dinners. So I'll e'en cobble first and put a touch to Father Francis' new sandals. Now to work. It's strange that a silly cobbler like me should join the brothers. A boozing, godless, melancholy cobbler, who thought a good shoe better than all the relics going. Then that quiet young man——

Enter a Peasant.

Good morning, my friend.

PEASANT.
Morning, father. Is Father Francis within?

JUNIPER.

No; he's on the hillside praying. There, is he not beautiful? What humility! What unction! It is a fine season for prayers, is the spring. Now, what for thee?

PEASANT.

I brought some firewood for the brothers.
[*Gives a bundle of sticks.*

JUNIPER.

Thou good, charitable soul. These logs will become prayers. But, lord a' mercy, you're half naked.

PEASANT.

Never mind that, father. I do have aches in my back from the cold, and all sorts of pains this bleak weather.

JUNIPER.

These spring days are cold. Would I could give thee my tunic! Father Francis has laid me under obedience not to give it away, or any part of my habit. But if thou wilt take it off my back I will not resist thee. Say nought, my son. Bless thee, bless thee, and good-bye.

PEASANT.

(Tain't much, but it's worth eight soldi.) The Madonna keep you, dear father. [*Exit.*

JUNIPER.

How much lighter I feel! I shall catch cold; so much the better. A sinful creature like me should not be so strong and well, while the other brothers have so many dolours.

Enter ELIAS.

Ah! Brother Elias, how you have sped.

ELIAS.

I have good news to tell.   The Bishop thinks
The proper time is come for us to ask
The Holy Father's sanction for our vows.

JUNIPER.

  The Holy Father? He won't see simple brothers
like us.

ELIAS.

Be not disturbed, good brother Juniper;
Live in your peaceful manner ; this is work
For wiser heads.   Is Francis in his cell ?

JUNIPER.

  Father Francis is out on the hillside. [*Exit* ELIAS.]
I hope no ill will come of this.

Enter a poor Woman.

WOMAN.

  Alms, for the love of God, my father. We are perished
for want of food.   My man has hurt his hand and
cannot work.   My little baby is sick.

JUNIPER.

  Poor thing, I am so sorry.   I have nothing.   Stay.
Wait a while.   There should be something on the
altar. [*Exit, and returns with a bit of hanging.*]
These bells are a superfluity.   Oh, thank me not.
Kiss thy baby for me.   I'll ask Brother Bernard to go
and see thy husband.   Poor thing! poor thing! [*Exit*
Woman.]   I wonder if I did wrong in giving away
these bells.   Father Francis told me to give nothing
without his permission.   Eh! that is his voice : I think
I'll come and sit by this rock.   There's less wind.

Enter FRANCIS *and* ELIAS.

FRANCIS.

Are we not powerful and recognized ?
A quiet monk in a retired cell
Might rule the world by prayer and never know
Himself to be a king ; the worth of us
Is not in human praise, however high ;
Deeds find their level.   Look upon the trees
Sitting in majesty, with vernal crowns
Upon their heads : they ask not to be known ;
'Tis not the forester who ticks them off
Who makes their stately height, but patient days
Of leaning to the sun, and peaceful nights
Of dewy sleep and unambitious dreams.
Thus let us grow ; we may be honest beams
To build the house of faith, or gird the ships
That breast the wearing of the stormy seas.

              [JUNIPER *sneezes and* FRANCIS *finding him*
                    hidden brings him out.

Who gave thee leave to sneeze on such a fine spring
day ? Where is thy tunic ?

JUNIPER.

A good man took it off my back and went away
with it.

FRANCIS.

Thou rememberest what I told thee ?

JUNIPER.

Yes.

FRANCIS.

And what else hast thou given away ?

JUNIPER.

Nothing.

FRANCIS.

Nothing at all ?

E

JUNIPER.

Nothing except certain little silver bells on a hanging of the grand altar. I gave them to a poor woman who had great need of them. Her husband has hurt his hand and cannot work; her little baby is sick.

FRANCIS.

Thou didst well to help her. I commend thee for thy charity. But thou hast been disobedient, and for that I must give thee a sound correction.

JUNIPER.

Dear Father Francis, I will first call the brothers, if I may; nothing is better for me than to have a good humiliation before them. [*Rings the bell.*] Brother John, Brother John, come and see Juniper properly corrected. Brother Masseo, Brother Ruffino, Brother Leo, come quickly. Brother Juniper has been disobedient; come and see him punished. Brother Sylvester, Brother Giles, come and hear Father Francis speak of obedience. Father, you must give me a sound correction of hard words to soften my wicked heart.

Enter the Brothers.

GILES.

Is Juniper in trouble again?

FRANCIS.

Giles, will you fetch me my new tunic? [*Exit* GILES.

LEO.

If Brother Juniper is to have a correction I pray you give me half his punishment.

FRANCIS.

My sons, it is well that you should hear what Brother Juniper has done. He has cut off the silver

bells from the hanging of the altar to give to a poor
woman whose child was sick.—What a noise the birds
make! it is as if they wished to join our colloquy.

Enter GILES.

I cannot hear myself speak. I pray you stay a
moment while I speak to them.
'Tis well ye praise your Maker, little birds ;
Praise Him in every hour and every place !
He gave you winged liberty to fly
In this illimitable gracious air ;
And for yourselves and for your offspring small
A twofold and a threefold garment wove,
Albeit ye neither spin nor sew. He sent,
When all the world was ocean in His rage,
Two of your ancestors into the ark,
That little birds might still be glad to sing.
He feeds you though you neither sow nor reap ;
He gives you founts and rivers for your thirst,
Mountains and valleys for to shelter you,
And trees wherein ye make your simple nests.
Be sure your Maker loves you very well,
Who gives such bounties to you. Little sisters,
I pray you hold ingratitude afar,
And study always to adore the Lord.

JUNIPER.
They are quite silent.

LEO.
How they open their beaks and stretch their necks !

JUNIPER.
See them flap their wings.

LEO.
They bow their heads to the ground.

FRANCIS.

What a multitude they make!   There is a swallow.

LEO.

What a sapient sparrow!

FRANCIS.

They are so familiar.
Dear Lord, we thank Thee for Thy little birds.
                    [*Makes the sign of the cross.*
Fly away, little sisters.

ELIAS.

They go all ways, east, west, south and north.
So will this order go by Heaven's will.

FRANCIS.

As little birds, and still possessing nothing,
Save wings to go where'er He wishes us,
Flying on tender providential airs,
And singing loud the glories of our Master.

JUNIPER.

Father Francis, you have forgotten my correction.

FRANCIS.

Put on this tunic, Brother Juniper.

JUNIPER.

It is your fine new tunic, Father Francis; 'tis much
too good for me; give me thy old one.   I want to be
humiliated.

FRANCIS.

I have corrected thee till I am quite hoarse, dear
brother.   What can I more?   Give me a little water.
                    [LEO *brings him water from the well.*

JUNIPER.

Oh! what a wicked man I am. He is quite hoarse
with weariness. I must find a remedy, I must find a
remedy.   [*Exit* JUNIPER.

FRANCIS.

I would I had a forest of such Junipers!
Tell me, is Brother Bernard yet returned?
Here is our brother as we speak of him.

Enter BERNARD.

How goes our patient?

BERNARD.
She is better now.

FRANCIS.
You are not weary, Brother Bernard?

BERNARD.
No,
If thou hast aught of work for me to do.
[*Exeunt the* Brothers.

FRANCIS.
Come, then, I have another task for thee.

Enter JUNIPER.

Yes, Juniper?

JUNIPER.

Father, I have considered the remedy for your hoarse-
ness, and have found this hasty-pudding for you. I
pray you eat of it; it will ease your throat and chest.

FRANCIS.

I thank you, my son, but have you cooked for the
brethren?

JUNIPER.

No.

FRANCIS.

Then I pray thee do thy cooking, for the brothers are hungry.

JUNIPER.

I pray you eat of my hasty-pudding at once ; it will do you good.

FRANCIS.

I have no time ; I must confer with Brother Bernard.
[*Exeunt* FRANCIS *and* BERNARD. *The silence
is broken by the water trickling from the
pail into the well.*

JUNIPER.

Yes, O water! thou mayest trickle down, drop by drop, but there's more thankful tears in my heart than ever water came out of thy well.

Enter CLARE, *alone.*

CLARE.

Is Father Francis to be seen ?

JUNIPER.

I will send him to you, sweet lady. I would I knew why she is come hither, and alone. But curiosity is a sin.   [*Exit* JUNIPER.

CLARE.

To thee these flowers, O Virgin mother mild !

Enter FRANCIS.

FRANCIS.

The Lady Clare is welcome.

CLARE.

You do know
My name, kind father?

FRANCIS.

More, I do await you.

CLARE.

Then may I plainly speak.   Your life and words
Have moved my heart, and if I might avail
To serve the holy cause of Poverty,
I wish to know how I may dedicate
Myself to it, and what the mode and rule
You would ordain, and what novitiate.

FRANCIS.

Fair maiden, you mistake.   There is no rule
Nor any making of a preparation
To follow Poverty.   All goodly deeds
Come of themselves in us.   The mighty sun
Asks not command to rise, nor does the wind
Wait for the word to blow, nor do the streams
Pause ere they dance into the thirsty plains,
Nor do the flowers inquire before they bloom:
There is a time for each, and unto thee
There is no need save God's necessity.

CLARE.

I am an ignorant and simple maid.

FRANCIS.

That is a merit in the works of God ;
What knowledge has the bird that sings His praise ?

CLARE.

To sing to God and tend upon His poor
Might be a woman's part.

FRANCIS.
                    Would she forego
The child that woman ever longs to bear?

CLARE.
The Holy Mother once did bear a babe,
There is no need that other babes should be.

FRANCIS.
Could she prolong her prayers the whole night
        through?

CLARE.
Out of her weakness would her prayers grow strong.

FRANCIS.
She could not leave the dear familiar hearth?

CLARE.
Can she forget the Heaven that is her home?

FRANCIS.
Is there a maid who loves not rich attire?

CLARE.
What finer vesture than humility?

FRANCIS.
The food of high-bred maids is delicate.

CLARE.
But mean it is to sacramental bread!
Oh, tempt me not, my father, with these things,
For they are little by my great desire.
It will be hard to meet my sire's regrets,
But else I have no fear except the Lord's.

FRANCIS.
And well I know it, and this day for me

Is hallowed by a woman's promises ;
Long hours of springtide calm have made me bold,
And I have prayed to have a blessing shown
Upon the brothers' holy strife, and thou
Art come, the certain answer to our prayers.

Enter BERNARD *and* ELIAS.

Brothers, this is our Sister Clare, who will take
to herself other sisters, and in St. Damien's live,
following Holy Poverty.

ACT III.

The court of the Convent of St. Damien's. CLARE *sits alone on a stone seat shaded by an olive tree ; to the right a road passing down into the valley.*

CLARE.

THE years go softly by and do not change
  My girlish gladness in my quiet life ;
This Poverty is a kind elder sister,
Who rules me by her love, and not her years,
For she is firm and wins obedience,
And she is merry when my thoughts are dull,
And in her homely aspect she is fair ;
Her eyes of grey are kind, and if her robe
Be bound with thorns, 'tis very white and pure.

Enter CONRAD.

Conrad !

CONRAD.

      Yes, Conrad come again to thee,
Conrad who loves thee still.

CLARE.

          Hush, hush, my friend.
Do you not see that I have taken vows ?

CONRAD.

And well that simple coif becomes your face !

CLARE.

I beg you to excuse—

CONRAD.
                My pretty Clare,
'Tis but a day that I have been at home—
We have been fighting by Pistoia's walls—
And hearing that your heart was still to win,
For you have not yet made your final vow
In an established order, no, nor will,
If a man's strenuous love can move your mind
From this fantastic life—and all do know
I loved you very dearly, and went forth
And made your name resound above the din
Of battle and the praise of other ladies ;
And I have won much honour for your scarf,
And bear on me the spurs my prowess won,
And I have found thee, and before thy feet
I put the loving prayer and worth of me,
Conrad the cavalier of Castelfior.

CLARE.
I am the bride of Christ.

CONRAD.
                Whose name be praised,
But never did that dear and stainless Lord,
Who holds all mortals in His fealty,
Intend to separate well-seeming loves.
If thou wert in a consecrated house
I would not proffer the least plaint to thee,
For my heart would be slain, and I would go
Beneath the gloomy portals of despair
And die a monk.
                CLARE.
                I cannot speak with you.

CONRAD.
I am no famous knight, but at the least
A decent gentleman of stainless honour,
Should counsel thee more wisely and more well

Than a mean scabby beggar, dressed in rags,
A recreant squire who tries to pilfer pity
By breaking of an honest father's heart,
And shunning the more noble cares of war.

CLARE.

Be careful how you speak of one who is
The father of whatever's good in me.

CONRAD.

But till he came you had some thought for me.
Do you remember how we led the dance
At old Count Adrian's house, and you were kind,
And friendly were your eyes, until there sneaked
This tatterling Francis in—fair is thy wrath !—
With his pale face and whining frantic tale,
To build anew St. Damien's ancient house,
And all the women in their silks and laces
Clustered about this wretched mendicant,
And when he went your eyes did follow him,
Grown sad and pensive, and aloof from me ?

CLARE.

What woman could withhold her interest ?
He brought with him his bride, sweet Poverty.

CONRAD.

But I do love thee, and the day is fair,
And sweet it is returned from battlefields
To look on thee, and in this summer noon,
When all things are afire and mildly give
Their bodies to increase, will not your heart
Admit the kindly general law that bids
The man and maiden love ?   My gentle Clare,
Resolve to love me, come away with me,
Come to thy noble father and declare
A troth to me, and on the joyous morrow
We will be wed amid our friends and servants,

And to my castle will I bear thee home,
And there attended as thy worth befits,
Thou shalt be loved and honoured ever more.

CLARE.

If I could break a vow I hold divine,
How could I give a promise of my life?
If I have hearkened to you, understand,
'Tis only for my pity that your task
Should prove all fruitless.   Let me counsel thee;
There's many a dainty maid who would be glad
To have thy homage.

CONRAD.
It is thee I love.

CLARE.

A love impossible.

CONRAD.
I've played the lover
Sleekly to-day, the next time that I come
I'll show the man.

CLARE.
That seems to veil a threat!
If you had loved the Clare who was your friend,
You never would have spoken in such wise.

CONRAD.

But I must have thee to my love, sweet Clare,
And I am strong and resolute of will.

CLARE.
And thus you let your passion rule your mind!

CONRAD.

I am acknowledged strong by all my friends,
And if I ever yet did set my mind
On anything, it always fell to me;

This is a love that I do more desire
Than aught which ever did determine me,
And if I cannot win thee worthily,
I'll get thee basely.

CLARE.
May Christ pardon thee !

CONRAD.
I've said my say.   I will retire, sweet Clare ;
Yet in the pauses of thy evening prayers,
Think you a little of your wedding robe.

[*Exit* CONRAD.

CLARE.
Tears ? yes, a few—pity perhaps for him
Whose honour is perverted by false love,
And for myself, who shrink and suffer pain
As does a rose leaf when it's rudely touched.
There ; I am strong again.   'Twere better not
Tell Francis of this thing, for many cares
Are on him, and our chivalric sweet saint
Would be much hurt therein.   Ah ! Conrad, Conrad,
The cavalier Conrad of Castelfior,
You think that women love the show of strength,
The clanking of the steel, the swelling throat,
The waving of the hand ?   Were I in the world
I'd make a school for lovers, and instruct them
That a calm bearing well reposed on power,
And a sweet deference to the ways of woman,
A pure devotion and a tender care,
Is the true way to win a woman's heart.

Enter PICA *as a Nun.*

Dear mother of our Francis !

PICA.
                        Pretty pet,
How young you look to-day !

CLARE.

To be the head
Of a grave sisterhood !

PICA.

But you have wept
Some tears this afternoon ?   Show me thy face.

CLARE.

Here is my face.   *[Puts back her hood.*

PICA.

Why did they cut your hair ?
I am sure the dear good God who spun its gold
Did never mean it to be maimed like this ;
Know you that I have saved a tress of it,
And tied it with the pretty childish curls
Of Francis.

CLARE.

What would he say to that ?

PICA.

I often think—if I may say such things—
My little Francis might have married you.
I know that he was humble by your side,
But he would have achieved an equal place
And won you for his bride—your two young hearts
So kindly do accord, and when ye speak
There is a charming silence in the air,
And when ye stand together, you so meek
And he so brave, it is no little pity
Ye may not kiss and swear a lasting troth.

CLARE.

Dear friend, you must not say——

PICA.

Why do you laugh ?

CLARE.

I will reprove thee if thou sayest more.

PICA.

Well, let the young live, and the old wait.

Enter FRANCIS *and* BERNARD.

FRANCIS.

Peace be to the ruler of St. Damien's! Mother dear !

CLARE.

You came so quietly we did not hear you. Will you sit with us? We are working awhile after the meditation.

FRANCIS.

It's mighty pleasant under your olive tree.

CLARE.

Whence come you, brothers? ·

BERNARD.

From Sienna.

Enter HELEN *and two* Nuns.

CLARE.

So soon away after your return from Rome ?

FRANCIS.

Is this little lady a novice ?

CLARE.

Not yet.
Know you, Francis, whom you have missed ?

FRANCIS.

The Lady Giacoma ?

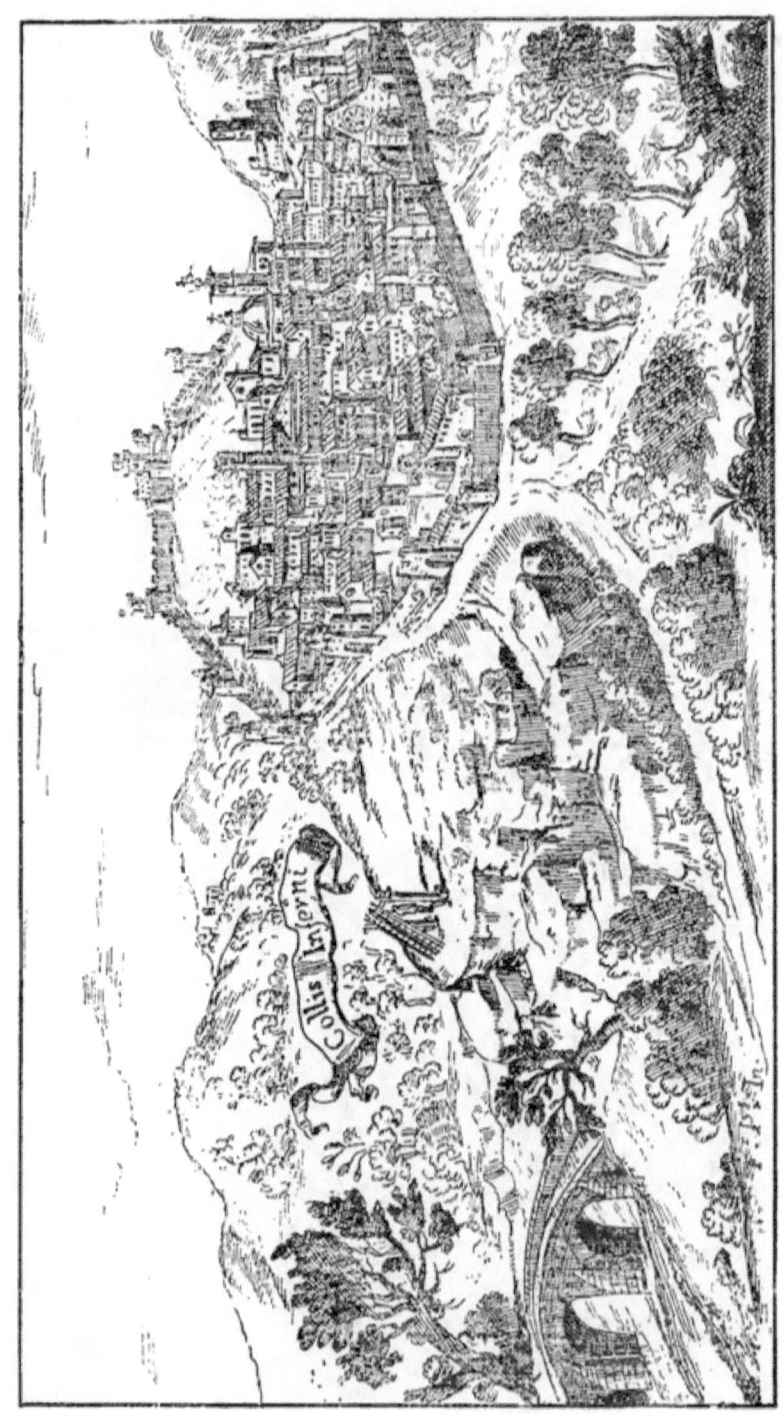

CLARE.
Yes, she left us three days ago.

FRANCIS.
Ah! the kind friend! How the brothers love her.

CLARE.
She wellnigh stole Juniper from them.

BERNARD.
Sister Pica, have you heard that Francis has made an exemplary conversion of a wolf that ravaged the town of Gubbio?

CLARE.
We know that he founded an order among the birds.

FRANCIS.
Fear not, my child, the wolf had a kind heart. I was once a wolf myself and prowled at night. But how are the doves we left with you, Sister Clare?

CLARE.
Oh, they are quite of us now; they are so familiar that they wake us up for matins.

FRANCIS.
Dear mother, ever watching tenderly?

PICA.
A mother's love is silent, dear my son.

BERNARD.
The sun is wellnigh set.

FRANCIS.
I will speak with Helen, and then we will continue our journey. [*The two* Nuns *make a reverence and retire.*

G

CLARE.

Yet first I pray you take a little supper;
You know you are not strong, the nights are cold.

FRANCIS.

Thanks, Sister Clare, we have no need to eat.

CLARE.

He still refuses—though it were not much
To let us show the hospitality
Of serving him.   Well, let the favour go ;
Yet I had wished to have this little joy.

BERNARD.

Francis, you do appear severe in this ;
She merely wishes once to eat with thee.
Did Sister Clare a greater grace request,
It were thy duty to accord it her.

FRANCIS.

You think, then, I should grant her this request ?

BERNARD.

'Tis meet you gratify her in this thing.

FRANCIS.

Then, child, we are so glad to be thy guests.

CLARE.

That is our good, kind Francis ; I am glad.
Our cakes are famous, he will eat of them.
Come, Helen.   [CLARE *and* HELEN *run out.*

FRANCIS.

          Sweet are scents of tender spring,
But not more sweet than women when they're true

And meek and holy ; were it not for them
This sinful world had perished long ago.

> [CLARE *and* HELEN *bring bread and cakes,*
> *water, and olives, and set them on the*
> *ground.*

FRANCIS [*Saying grace*].
We eat and drink to Thy glory, most dear Lord !

BERNARD.

Amen.

FRANCIS.

I often think the hour wherein we eat
Is very edifying ; in this bread
Most kindly sweet monitions do abide.

> [*Breaks bread and puts it on the ground.*

The house and hearth where ancient people dwelt
Fall to decay ; little remains to us
Of all that was familiar to them,
Save that the bread they ate with lowly thanks
Was of a corn no different to that
Which grows from the same earth to the same sun ;
The water that they drank was of the spring
That flows to-day.   Thus in our daily bread
We eat with our forefathers, and are met
With the old time.

> [*Raises bread to his mouth, but lays it down*
> *untasted.*

Our speeches and our dress,
The days and nights, are various with the climes ;
Only at noon and at the set of sun,
However that may rise or this may fall,
The unnumbered dwellers of the whole wide earth
Eat bread, drink water, some in nature's make,
And others with absurd contrivances
Of their pure savours into foolish tastes,
But bread and water still.   There is in this
A kind communion with our fellow-men,

Where'er they be ; and tender is the thought
Of the foregathering of young and old,
Father and wife and child and serving-man,
To satisfy the hunger earned of toil.
                              [*Putting aside the bread.*
Yet there's in this another sacredness,
Because our gentle Lord ate earthly food,
Knew earthly hunger.   Often at the eve,
In the sun-wasted, grace-abounding plains,
He and His dear disciples sat together,
Engrossed in wondrous conversations,
And holy jests, and solemn silences.
Thus when we eat we are with good men past,
And good men living, and undying Heaven.
                              [*Says grace.*
We are most thankful to thee, O Lord, for this
banquet, and do bless Thy name.

CLARE.
But you have eaten nothing.

FRANCIS.
Truly ? I hunger no more.

BERNARD.
And I also am filled ; such nourishment there is in
moral considerations.

FRANCIS.
Little Helen, will you walk with me ?
                    [*Exeunt* FRANCIS *and* HELEN.

CLARE.
Brother Bernard, you should take better care of
our Francis.   He still has his cough ; he looks pale.
These journeys are easy to you, but perilous to him.
See that he sleeps not in open places, let him not walk

too long, make him eat at proper hours. You must
think more of him.

PICA.

But, Sister Clare, he is their treasure.

CLARE.

Then let them learn wisdom from a woman to pre-
serve their treasure.

BERNARD.

You forget that other people besides yourself do
love him.

CLARE.

If you love him well, you can care for him better.
You promise me, Brother Bernard?

BERNARD.

I promise you, Sister Clare.

Enter FRANCIS *and* HELEN.

FRANCIS.

Helen prefers to wait a little while before she takes
her novitiate.

Enter CECCO *with his two sons.*

Bless us, 'tis friend Cecco.

CECCO.

Father Francis and Sister Clare!

FRANCIS.

"Piping fresh and piping clear?" Namesake, if
thou growest so thin thou'lt pine away.

CECCO.

He, he!

FRANCIS.

And how's Mina and the baby?

CECCO.

Rarely, Father Francis. And, Father Francis, I won't be denied. When I heard that beast Jacopo was in jail—bad luck to him for his bad pipe-playing!—I said to myself, I'll give Father Francis a double penny.

FRANCIS.

I'll take it if thou'lt do something for me. This very night thou art to go to the jail window and call for Jacopo, and be reconciled to him. Oh, so you won't? [CECCO *shakes his head.*] Thou need'st not come to pipe to me again, Cecco.

CECCO.

He'll think I come a-mocking.

FRANCIS.

Then give him this double soldo from me. Yes, you'll do it to please Sister Clare.

CLARE.

You play so much better than Jacopo, you ought to be generous.

CECCO.

'Tis hard on a man that he may not hate his enemies.

FRANCIS.

'Tis sweet to a man that he can love them. Friend Cecco, I, too, mean to be thy rival. [*He picks up a bit of wood and a stick.*] I'll play on the viol to ye. Here's for a dance. [*He dances, and is followed by* CECCO.] Come, Bernard, dance with us.

[FRANCIS *takes* CECCO *by the waist.*

CECCO.

Ah ! father Francis, have mercy on a fat man.

FRANCIS.

One fling more ; to it, Cecco, to it, Cecco ; I am
spent. [*They sit down exhausted.*

CECCO.

Had you taken to pipe-playing, father, there would
have been little chance for us.

FRANCIS.

Nay, friend Cecco, each man to his task.

CLARE.

Now dies the day, while soft religious bells
Make it a requiem ; the sounds of toil
Have ceased upon the plain, and all the herds
Secure are housed. The gnarlèd olive trees
Take cloaks of mist and sleep, the runnel waters
Subdue their babble, and the wayside flowers
Nestle upon their grassy pillows green.

Enter ELIAS.

FRANCIS.

How dark the shadows fall ! [*Turning.*
Is't you, Elias ?

ELIAS.

I heard that you were seen upon the way,
And hastened to attend you.

FRANCIS.

It is well,
How go the brothers ?

ELIAS.

As poor sinners may.

FRANCIS.

Good-night, dear mother. [*Exit* PICA.] Will you
pipe us down into the valley, Cecco?

CECCO.

Lads, we're going to play the good brothers a bit
on their journey.

FRANCIS.

Good-bye then, Sister Clare; good-bye, little Helen.
[CLARE *and* HELEN *kneel to his blessing.*
FRANCIS, BERNARD, ELIAS, *and the
players descend into the valley.* CECCO
begins to pipe.

FRANCIS.

Not yet, friend Cecco.   Good-bye, Sister Clare.

CLARE.

Good-bye.   *[Sounds of retiring voices.*

HELEN.

Is that Father Francis?

CLARE.

He is most simple, is he not, my dear?
And not a hero as we dream of them
When we are young.   *[A piping heard.*
He frightened you at first,
Yet you ere long will learn to love him too,
And seek him for your truest, wisest friend,
And more than father.   There is nursed in him
Such sympathy of understanding love,
And such resource of gentleness, that all
Who cross his path are in their love renewed.
The timid birds, the angry hunted beasts,
Forget their instinct to devour or fly
When they approach him; men of hardest heart

Or meanest temper spring regenerate,
When he has shamed their cruelties or fears,
And take his qualities.　　　　[*The piping ends.*
　　　　　　　　He is a sun
That lights the life it gives, and makes us fruitful
In whatsoever things we have to bear.
The moon shines on us ; we, with lesser light
Reflected from our Francis, still may give
Continuance to his work, and soothe the world
Weary of toil, and soiled by stain of sin,
With the kind beams of womanly intercession,
And the chaste plea of our devoted lives.
　　　　　　　　[*Exeunt* CLARE *and* HELEN.

　　　　　HYMN. [*Within.*]
　　Virgin of all virgins, hail,
　　　　Hail, sweet star of eve ;
　　The poor labourer come to rest
　　　　Kind thou dost receive ;
　　Help thou hast for sordid wights
　　　　Who toward ruin fare ;
　　To thy daughters' lowly sleep,
　　　　Mother, give thy care.
　　[*While these words are being sung the sky
　　　　grows dark and* CONRAD *enters with men
　　　　bearing a ladder, which they put against
　　　　the shutters of the dormitory of the Con-
　　　　vent. All is silent and* CONRAD *pauses
　　　　in indecision, then mounts the ladder,
　　　　when a distant horn is heard to sound,
　　　　and a man drops his sword on the stones.
　　　　The shutters open from within, and in a
　　　　strange light* CLARE *is seen with the
　　　　sacramental pyx in her hand,* CONRAD
　　　　falls from the ladder, men cry out and
　　　　three foresters run in and disperse the
　　　　marauders and seize* CONRAD, *who lies
　　　　groaning on the ground.*

　　　　　　　　H

ACT IV.

The chapel of the Porziuncula surrounded by snow ; the
night is falling. FRANCIS *enters with* BERNARD,
and meets ELIAS *coming from the Chapel.*

FRANCIS.

ELIAS, as there has been some report
   Of an attack upon St. Damien's,
Some months agone, I wish it to be published
That the intruder now has paid the debt,
And miserably died.   Our Sister Clare
Had nursed him in the cottage where he lay,
Lingering till the falling of the snows.

ELIAS.

'Tis said that he was climbing in by night
Till by the foresters surprised, who seized him.

FRANCIS.

Nay ; Sister Clare heard an unwonted noise,
And, taking in her hand the sacrament,
Spurned the mean coward ere assistance came.

BERNARD.

This Conrad loved our Clare, or thought to love her,
If such an impious passion can be love.

FRANCIS.

We buried him to-day.

ELIAS.
        How was his death ?

FRANCIS.

His death was piteous ; but he had repented.

ELIAS.

The tale is very strange.

BERNARD.
And sorrowful.

ELIAS.

The tale is very strange——

FRANCIS.
Is very strange?

ELIAS.

Why was he nursed by Sister Clare, not us?

FRANCIS.

The Sister Clare was fearful of our wrath
Against the man, and only when his sickness
Grew mortal, she required our offices.

ELIAS.

And she had nursed him all the summer through?

FRANCIS.

What do you mean?

ELIAS.
'Tis not for me to speak.

FRANCIS.

Speak, in the name of your obedience!

ELIAS.

When first these women came into the order
I knew there would be harm.   Women are weak,
Fitful and vain, and by their gentler lives

Assist the devil's snares, and in their pity
Console a passion till it takes a hold
Upon their hearts.   And are we well assured
That Clare, who outwardly is most devout,
Is free from blame in this ?   The holy life
Has sometimes covered sin ; it is our duty
To watch upon each other ; at the least
It was unwise for Clare to take this charge.

FRANCIS.

I am assured of this, if any of us
Can speak such doubts, and impudently accuse
A gentle life, of utter innocence,
There is an end to any brotherhood.
Get thee away and pray until the dawn
That thou may'st be as pure as Sister Clare.

ELIAS.

Forgive me my suspicions ; I have erred
In thinking evil where no evil is.
I'll pray that what I thought may not be true,
And that all evils may be kept from us.
                    [*Exit* ELIAS *into the Chapel.*

BERNARD.

That's like a curse ; thus in the Afric wilds
I've seen a serpent slant its head and hiss,
And being afraid to sting, slowly retire.

FRANCIS.

These things are hard to bear.   Ah, brother Bernard,
Full often looking through our present plenty
I see a famine coming, and I fear.
The marks of favour of the Holy See,
The bringing of the heathen to the fold,
The reconciliation in the town,
Are all good things, but how shall they avail,
If mutiny is in our house ?   The times

Of intimate love seem gone from us ! we go
So many ways ; 'tis not the unison
Of a few hearts whose every rise and fall
Sang sweet in comrade love of our Lord Christ.
Yes, often you console me in my cares,
But you are weary, Bernard.   Go and rest.
Good-night, may angels watch thee in thy sleep.

[*Exit* BERNARD.

Lustrous, dear, immaculate, white snow,
Thinking no evil, covering the ground
Against the cold, and keeping soft and warm
The seeds that shall be harvest, cool my brow ;
Thou never wilt accuse thy sister water,
Or brother fire.   Ah ! my poor Elias,
Misled by ignorance, I think, not malice,
You blame our Clare ?   There was a sting in his
    words !
A father has a natural jealousy
To see his daughter loved.   I cannot put
The thought from me : that is the special harm
Of evil speech.   This Conrad I remember
Was a brave-looking knight, whom any maid—
But I am thinking evil.   Francis, Francis,
Slander not with Elias, rise with Clare
To the true reverence that knows not guile !
I'll go and help Elias in his prayers ;
My heart is sick.—What ?   I am not myself.
What is it glimmers by the snow-clad thorn ?

Enter CLARE.

CLARE.

O Francis, I am glad that you are sound,
Safe, and well.   The horrors of this death
Have much perturbed me, and I came as borne
By an imperious wind to see thy face ;
Give me thy blessing and I will go home.

FRANCIS.

I too have been disturbed, yet I should chide thee.

CLARE.

Reprove me for my fears, for in your voice
I take new courage——

FRANCIS.

　　　　Which you might have asked
Of One who hears——

CLARE.

　　　Have I offended, Francis?

FRANCIS.

The night is very cold, you must not stay.

CLARE.

Francis, there's something on your mind to-night.

FRANCIS.

You are no more a child; I'll plainly speak.
Sometimes by charity we cause to stumble,
And as men's thoughts are ever prone to take
A base interpretation, it is said
Your woman's care for Conrad till his death
Concealed a love for him.

CLARE.

　　　　Francis, you know me!

FRANCIS.

I know you, Clare, but others may not know.
I still commend thee for thy generous deed,
But you have erred in not informing us.

CLARE.

I am not strong enough to walk alone,
And must rely on thee—O God, my God!

FRANCIS.

You are not ill.

CLARE.

No—but I must go home.

FRANCIS.

You do not doubt yourself—for evil words
Oft bring us to suspect our purest acts.

CLARE.

I know I loved not Conrad.   Hush, who comes?
> [*The door of the Chapel opens.* FRANCIS
> *motions to* CLARE, *who goes into the
> shadow.*

Enter SYLVESTER.

You have had blessing to your prayers to-night!

SYLVESTER.

I have had a most comfortable prayer, dear father.
Give me thy blessing.

FRANCIS.

Thus do I give it thee.   [*Kneels and kisses his hand.*
Now give me yours.

SYLVESTER.

May Christ keep thee, husband of Poverty.
> [*Exit* SYLVESTER.

FRANCIS.

Husband of Poverty!

CLARE.

But why did you conceal me?

FRANCIS.

Could we fear
The eye of man?

CLARE.

'Tis that we love each other.

FRANCIS.

That we do love ?—
It is the raving of the man that's dead
That lingers in your ears, and hurts your thoughts.

CLARE.

Then look me in the eyes.

FRANCIS.

'Tis true, we love.

CLARE.

Thou ever hast been master of my heart,
Hast been with me in spirit night and morn,
And I have waited for thy welcome step,
And seen thy face upon my crucifix,
And felt thy soothing hand upon my hair.
Yet only thought of thee as of a father—
But—may I be forgiven !—in these hours
Of watching by the bed and hearkening
To the reiteration of my name
In yearning accents cried—I must have come
To think it would be sweet to hear that love,
Spoken by one I held in reverence,
And though unknown in me, deep, deep it lay,
The question, and the longing, and my heart
Waited for something, what, it could not tell.

FRANCIS.

Thus years of vain and petty incidents
Are gathered in a torrent, and our feet
Are shaken in their hold on solid ground.
When I gave up the world's last vanity
And stood i' the market-place a public mock,
'Twas thou didst pass, a child, and in my mind
The first sweet yearning of young love upsprung,

Unnoticed then, yet by its difference
Giving intensity to my despair ;
And when you came to be the bride of Christ,
Here in this very place that Easter morn,
And all the freshly-bloomèd woods did ring
With joyous hymns of welcome, I was grave,
Distraught and malcontent, I knew not why ;
And when before the fiery Soldan's troops
We scarce escaped cruel barbaric death,
It was thy name that lingered on my lips
And made death sad.

CLARE.
But now we know ourselves.

FRANCIS.
It is a bitter thing that we should love.

CLARE.
We must not blame, but meekly take the burden
That's set upon us.   We will learn to bear it.

FRANCIS.
Nor ever did I know that love was this;
We were two children born into a world
We scarce perceived, and ere our thoughts were grown
Even to stand on tiptoe and look out
To know what things there are to be enjoyed,
Suffered, or hoped for, we had chosen our lives,
And now we stand and see.

CLARE.
Beneath the Cross.

FRANCIS.
And must we ever sorrow in its shade ?
Hath not the Prophet sung it in his rede,
Shall not the voice of weeping turn to joy,

I

And we inhabit the fair house we build,
And planting vineyards eat the fruit of them ;
And there be naught of labour done in vain,
Nor children born to perish, nor the elect
Be punished for the sinner, nor the ungodly
Sit in the place of power and order ill,
Nor there be any drawing of the sword
Upon the holy mountains ?   For the dawn
Must chase the night, and hatred be ashamed,
And the high citadel of hell thrown down !
Have not the righteous lives of sacrifice,
That fought with the eternal for its palm,
Achieved deliverance ?   Have not the saints
And much-enduring martyrs brought the reign
Of heaven upon the earth, and may not we
In innocence of heart possess the kingdom
And recreate the race that walked with God ?

CLARE.

The air is full of bells, and on the trees
Red roses hang, while mystical sweet scents
Are wafted o'er the snow, and songs are made,
And this should be the garden, Paradise.

FRANCIS.

Kiss me, dear love, give me thy mouth to kiss ;
Our bridal bed is strewn by angel hands,
Love bears the veil, the stars attend on us,
Who lovingly will make the world anew.
        [*They bend forward to kiss but start back in
                    horror.*
Oh no, the Cross is not to be redeemed,
And men must still come lowly, wearing weeds,
And with their anguish and their tears anoint
The cruel wounds of Christ still crucified.

CLARE.

How did we come to this ?

FRANCIS.
The heart of man

Is never thoroughly cleansed.   O God, that we
Should be each other's peril !

CLARE.
Dost forgive me ?

FRANCIS.

We share the shame.

CLARE.
Then let us help each other,

To cast it from us.

FRANCIS.
We have lived in a dream.

And did we think the tempter would not plot
'Gainst our salvations ?   He was not dismayed
Because we could resist a cup of wine,
Nor fell by gluttony nor sloth nor malice ;
He snared us in the joy of gentleness,
The kindly opportunities of love.
Yet the avoidance was not difficult.
What right have we to joy ?   We are too poor.

CLARE.

What must we do ?

FRANCIS.
I am not fit to rule ;—

And heavenly wisdom has a judge prepared.
[*Goes to the Chapel door and calls.*

Elias, Elias, prithee come to me.

Enter ELIAS.

ELIAS.

Clare, I have wronged thee in my thoughts, I know.

FRANCIS.

O stay—listen to me.   There was a man

Who sought a bride, and by a happy chance
Found one who did excel in every way,
Loving and wise, and patient and sincere,
A thrifty housewife—how could she be else?
For she was Poverty.   He married her,
And certain offspring did they have, whose love
Was more than blessing.   When some quiet years
Had passed, with never faintest cloud of grief
Or of misunderstanding, came a maid
So charitably gentle, fair, and meek,
That Poverty grew jealous ; she was old,
The other young ; and she was hoarse of voice,
The other had most merry sound of speech ;
Her feet with difficulty went the way,
The other tripped as lightly as the brooks ;
And Poverty, to prove her husband's truth,
Besought him, whether he should love or no
The other maid, to see her face no more.
He for his love to his wife Poverty
Must needs obey, and, following her will,
Learns that he loves the maid and not the wife.

ELIAS.

Is Francis sick?

CLARE.
Is not the story clear?

ELIAS.
Then is our order perished.

FRANCIS.
Nay, not so.
But thou must rule it.

ELIAS.
I must rule the order?
I have not the authority you wield.

FRANCIS.

You are not weakened by the bonds I bear.

ELIAS.

But you are free from actual taint of wrong,
The vile abomination and the sin?
But answer me!

FRANCIS.

        Thou dost not doubt, Elias?
That we have to our souls done grievous wrong
Is manifest, but more—it could not be.

ELIAS.

Ye are agreed to part?

CLARE.

        This very night.

FRANCIS.

But I must be abased before her eyes:
Take now my cord, and scourge me.

CLARE.

              Must this be?

ELIAS.

What profit hast thou if thy body's scourged?
It is thy soul that merits punishment.

FRANCIS.

What should I do?

ELIAS.

        To spurn this earthly love
Are you resolved to suffer once for all?

FRANCIS.

I am, I am indeed.

ELIAS.

        Then—scourge the woman.

FRANCIS.

Not that, not that !

CLARE.
Francis, 'tis necessary.
For both shall suffer with a mutual pain
For the offence that both have nourished.

ELIAS.
You will not prove your loyalty to God ?

FRANCIS.
Surely I love my Master more than thee ;—
This be the token of our penitence.
> [*He undoes his knotted cord, while* CLARE
> *kneels and bares her shoulders.   He twice
> raises the cord.*

CLARE.
May heaven give thee strength to use the cord.
> [FRANCIS *flings the cord away.*

FRANCIS.
I cannot do it.   Let the struggle end ;
The full remainder of our severed lives
Must do the task.

ELIAS.
Endeavour once again.

Enter JUNIPER *with a lantern.*

JUNIPER.
Father Francis and Sister Clare and Brother Elias
all intent on religious delights, still plotting good for
the brothers and sisters, whether in sunshine or snow.

FRANCIS.
I ever loved our lowly sister snow.

JUNIPER.

I had a game of snowballs with the boys to-day.
I pelted 'em finely.   But I must not stay talking.

ELIAS.

And we perhaps are here for penitence.

JUNIPER.

Penitence for you !   The angels are friends to Father
Francis, at least, and Sister Clare.   Have you com-
mitted an error, Brother Elias ?

ELIAS.

We all are tempted, Brother Juniper.

JUNIPER.

Now I have discovered a very excellent way to
avoid diabolical suggestions, for when the tumult
approaches I run and close the door of my heart and
hoist up the portcullis, and occupy myself with severe
meditations, so when the enemy comes and knocks at
the door, I answer, as it were from within, " Begone,
for the Castle is full already and can hold no more
guests," and this thwarts the besieger, so that he de-
parts, not only from me, but from all the country
round.   Good-night.

FRANCIS.

Leave us your lantern, Brother Juniper.

JUNIPER.

Burn bright, lantern, 'tis to light Sister Clare.
                                        [*Exit* JUNIPER.

ELIAS.

Now must ye part.

CLARE.

Oh, must we part so soon ?

FRANCIS.

One thing I ask, but only as a plea.

ELIAS.

One thing I grant, but straightway must ye part.

FRANCIS.

Bear her home—but do not speak to her.

[CLARE *goes to* FRANCIS.

ELIAS.

Ye must not say farewell.   Ye shall be dead
One to another.

CLARE.

It is better so.

ELIAS.

You, Francis, wait for me till I return.
For as I humbly did obey your will
When you were my superior, I must ask
That you obey me as implicitly
Now that I am superior over you.

[*Exit* CLARE *with* ELIAS.

FRANCIS.

Not blows, nor tears, nor lifelong litanies
Shall calm this rebel fever; I must go
Into the wastes, be far removed from man,
And give the fervour of my agonies
To God's desire.   'Tis grievous O my Lord,
If I may still come near thy hallowed name,
That our united strength is lost to thee.

O simple Francis, could'st thou dream of wife and
child ?   Fool, thou art too poor.

[*He piles up blocks of snow to make grotesque
shapes.*

This is my mate, a fair cold lady, who'll not heed
me ; these my children.   She goes in the pale dawn
over the frozen stones.—Oh, no ! I may not think on it.
I am too poor even to pity her, O bride of snow.

ACT V.

SCENE I. *The garden of the Convent of St. Damien's ;
on the wall a Crucifix.* FRANCIS, *reclining, speaks
with* CLARE ; *a lily is between them.*

FRANCIS.

IS it so many years since we did part,
   Yet nothing here is changed, and only I
Returning show the passing of the years ?
Thus at the night the labourer cometh home
And sits awhile, ere going in to rest,
Considering the fulness of his toil.

CLARE.

And thou art satisfied with what is done ?

FRANCIS.

Alas for me ! My children disobey
The simple rule I gave them ; they begin
To build them monasteries, and make store
Of worldly goods. They look on me
More as a relic now than as a man :
A paring of my nails, a scrap of hair,
Almost my breaths are envied, and my end
Is eagerly foretold and waited for.
And, finally, of the unearthly signs
I took upon the Mount Alvernia,
They, if my resolution were not firm,
Would make a peepshow for the gaping crowd.

CLARE.

Many a vain report has come to me

Of this event, and I as yet misknow
What it portends, and how it may read.

FRANCIS.

I may not tell thee, even thee, my friend.
That I do on me bear the ultimate seals,
The marks of nails upon my hands and feet,
A wound as of a lance within my side,
This must suffice thee ; more I may not tell.

CLARE.

It is enough to know thou bearest them.

FRANCIS.

I bear those marks.

CLARE.
Then I am satisfied.

FRANCIS.

The brothers are not satisfied, and give
The story, as in vain imagining
They think it should have come to pass, as if
Aught holy could be known to those who have
Deserted Poverty.   They are my fruits—
Perhaps the blossom always is most fair,
And fruit to go into the use of men
Must lose the delicate scent and soft-flushed hue
That was so lovely and so promising,
And such a pleasure to the father tree.
Ah ! when the tree is old, and worn, and sick,
And trembles on the ground, and feels the cold
Creep into his sad body, it is hard
To know his fruit half-rotted on the bough,
And that his best is fallen from his reach,
Forgetful even to ingratitude.
But ever in such case there will remain
One cluster that is worthy of his pride
And reconciles him to his near decay.

CLARE.

I was powerless to help thee as I would.

FRANCIS.

Yet have you ever helped since we parted.
Has the time been very weary with you, Clare?

CLARE.

Most have I suffered for thy suffering ;
Yet was my courage holpen and upheld.
I had thy mother for my consolation ;
She, ere we knew it, knew we loved each other,
And till she died, was as a mother to me ;
And in the daily round monotonous,
And with some sternness for my weaker moods,
And for the knowledge that I fought with you,
My tears were dried, and in my chastened heart
My love for thee was to my love for Christ
A lowly servitor ; it was the earth
Wherein the bright eternal lily bloomed.

FRANCIS.

But thou, sweet, art a saint, a blessed saint.

CLARE.

Was there this need for us to be apart ?

FRANCIS.

I am a man, and could not bear to look
Daily upon the woman that thou art,
Could not have heard thee speak or seen thee move,
Could not have come to thee nor gone from thee,
Without such great devouring pangs of heart,
That to keep from thee was my only course ;
Whether by fuller knowledge and thy aid
I might have made my passion serviceable
And pure as thine, I know not ; I must think
This pain of absence excellent and kind

And useful.   In th' unrolling of my years
I chiefly bless the pains ; I see, I see
They were the sign-posts and directing spears
To the desired land.   I thank my God
That He has thought me worthy to be foiled,
Mocked, tempted, snared, deceived.
Oh, take me, scourge me, shame me, dearest Lord !
Cast me out upon the thorniest seas,
Whelm me in fiery-mouthed rocks,
Whatsoe'er thou wilt I'll suffer,
Born, living, dying, dead,
Perinde ad cadaver.   [*He sinks down.*

CLARE.

And much thou hast endured, alone, unloved !

FRANCIS.

And yet to me thy love has been repose
And cheer and refuge !   I can leave my task,
I know that one will ever faithful be,
And gathered into thy remembering heart
My purposes shall prosper and go on,
And not be lost.   I will not give to thee
Any direction for the sisters here.
Thy love will teach thee.   Love is very wise ;
Before we speak he hears, and ere he sees
Has understood !   Thy love completes my life
And soothes my end, and in my love of thee
Thou wilt be sheltered and accompanied ;
'Tis but a little while we meet again.
And now to say farewell.

CLARE.
            To say farewell?

FRANCIS.
Yet 'tis not parting, for my soul shall watch
Thee in thy lonely world and single task.

CLARE.

Is all hope gone ? The end so very near ?

FRANCIS.

'Twas but my hope to see thee and to die
At home, that made the careful angel pause.

CLARE.

May I not nurse thee for thy last dear days,
And do my little for thee, tender heart?

FRANCIS.

I, loved by thee, shall have thee near to me,
But wert thou present there are evil thoughts——

CLARE.

It is not God who separates us now ;
'Tis those for whom thou gavest all thy days.

FRANCIS.

I still have the affection of the few
Who following first will love me to the last.

CLARE.

Only I would some woman's hand might tend you.
Could you not send to our friend Giacoma ?

FRANCIS.

Pray then for her and she will surely come.
Farewell, farewell.

CLARE.

Give me some little thing
That you have borne upon you for remembrance.

FRANCIS.

I will enjoin on them to bring to you
This cross that lay upon my dying breast.

CLARE.

Thy love is very tender.   Ever kind
Thou wast to me, O father of my faith!
My thoughts have never wavered from thy side,
And ever will I keep thee in my heart,
Thy gentleness, thy laughter, thy commands,
Thy wishes spoken and thy purposes,
The love thou gavest me, dear heart, dear heart!

FRANCIS.

Weep not, my child! consider me as dead;
My love, 'tis only for a little while;
Now I am dead I lose so many pains;
I could not long go on to bear the load,
And death released me.   And for thee, my love,
I could not kiss thee as I longed to do,
But ere I went I left a kiss for thee,
                    [*He kisses the crucifix on the wall.*
Upon the feet of our Lord crucified.
Thus at the throne of love our lips had met;
            [*He puts his hand on her head as she bends to
                    kiss the crucifix.*
Our earthly love denied was given to God,
And taken up into His pitying bosom
Became a treasure safely kept for us,
Till when thou come and Love be all in all.
                    [*He falls in a swoon.*

SCENE 2.   *A turning in the road in front of
    Assisi.   A procession:* FRANCIS *borne on a litter
    by his* Monks; Citizens *and* Soldiers, *and* Children
    following.

FRANCIS.

Here set me down, I have to say farewell.
I should have thought the partings I have taken
These latter days had emptied out the vials

Of tears, and none remained to me to give
To skies or trees or stones which once were dear ;
Yet now I see thy youthful face, Assisi,
And pass thy pleasant lands, I seem to feel
As though I left a friend.   O, little town,
Set high upon thy hill, and guarded well
By th' elephantine big Subasio,
And by the stream Tupino, many times
Have I come up to thee, and paused to mark
How much of good strong walls and gardens fair
And blessed churches were in thee !   Thy ways
Go everywhere, into the sunny plain,
And on the mighty mountains, for thou hast
Sweet habitable spots for gentle work,
And lonely places meet for solemn prayers ;
Thou art the brightest gem of Italy,
For Umbria is Italy's best plain,
And thou the plain's most stately precious town,
And Umbria's brightest star.   Oh, could I now
Put my two arms about thy neck and press
A kiss upon thy forehead !   Thus I bless thee,
May all thy citizens be brave and kind,
Thy women fair and true, as ever yet
They have been found, and may thy city stand
Set far above decay, and rage, and wrath,
Or vile oppression ; may thy streets and rooms
Be full of heavenly songs and goodly joy,
And thou still holy, bountiful, and free !

My brothers, I have in this moment found my place
of burial.   There on the Mount of Hell lay my bones,
beneath the gibbets, that the poor felons may have a
comforter.   Now go on.

THE PEOPLE.

Behold the Saint, behold the Saint !

FRANCIS.

I do implore you, say not that.   It hurts me.   Take
me hence.   [*The procession passes.*

SCENE 3.   *The hut of* FRANCIS *adjoining the Porziun-*
  cula.   The Brothers *stand without.* SYLVESTER
  comes out with the sacrament, and in answer to a
  mute inquiry shakes his head. ELIAS *follows him.*

ELIAS.

Keep him within, I pray you.   He desires
To issue, and I fear his fevered brain
May make him play some folly ere he dies.
                              [*Calls a* Soldier.
What is your news?

SOLDIER.
              I went as I was bid,
And told them that we would not let them come,
As we desired to keep our saints ourselves,
And would have no one sniffing round their bones.

ELIAS.

Foligno then should give no further trouble.
Have you set watches in the several towns?

SOLDIER.

I have had full reports.   There is some talk,
But no one seems to know the end's so near.

ELIAS.

I thank you; here's your pay and something more;
Keep a good watch, and at the slightest sign
Come straight to me.

SOLDIER.
              I surely will, my father;
Give me your blessing.

ELIAS.

Eh?   Is that the doctor?
Good-day to you, I pray you come at once.
    [ELIAS *and the* Doctor *go in.   Voices are*
        heard ; the Brothers *press forward to*
        listen.   The Doctor *comes out.*

FRANCIS [*Within*].

Let me go out into the pleasant day,
I pray you let me rise.   Be not so hard.
I'm very ill ; you should be kind to me.
                    [*They bring him out.*
What joy to die upon the flower-sweet grass!
Sit by me, brothers ; there's no need to kneel.
The solemn offices of death are done.
How the birds fly!   I soon shall have my wings.
What is the time of day?   The sun's too bright.

BERNARD.

'Tis almost at the setting of the sun.

FRANCIS.

I thought 'twas noon—I—I am rather hoarse.
Hast not a hasty-pudding, Juniper?

JUNIPER.

  If a thousand lives of mine would make one hasty-
pudding, thou should'st have it.

FRANCIS.

Take off my clothes ; I wish to leave my vows
As I came into them, without a rag
Or anything that I can call my own.

ELIAS.

Hast thou not had enough of poverty?

FRANCIS.

That's true ; perhaps I have been somewhat stern.

Poor brother body, I have hurted thee
Too much, perhaps, for thou wast sick and frail,
Yet never didst complain, but meekly took
All my imperious spirit set on thee ;
Now comes thy rest and kind deliverance.
I pray you set my brother body free,
And take away these clothes that hamper him.

[They take off his tunic.

Sister Death,
I see thee hovering,
Long I waited for thee.

Bernard, art thou there? Leo and Juniper and
Sylvester? I wish all to love Brother Bernard. I
commend him to you to love and to honour as you
have me ; let all the brothers take counsel of him
even as they have with me. Brother Leo, I bless
thee, my little lamb of God! Brother Sylvester, my
father and priest! Brother Juniper, kiss me. Elias,
seek not to act too much against my intentions. [ELIAS
weeps.] Oh, I know thou lovest me ; yet do I fear for
thee and these.

BERNARD.

Bless also all thy brothers near and far.

FRANCIS.

I bless them wheresoever they may be,
And also those who shall be of our vows
In the late years unto the ages' ends.
Would I could see them and commune with them,
And lay my hands on their devoted heads!
Who is it comes? Let them approach, Elias.

Enter the LADY GIACOMA *with her* Children *and*
Retinue.

GIACOMA.

Warned by a dream, my father, I have come
To nurse thy dying days, and have thy blessing.

FRANCIS.

I am very glad.

GIACOMA.

Tomaso, bring a little water here.

[*She props him up.*

There, he is easier.   Let me cool thy brow.
Is this the way you nurse your dying father ?

FRANCIS.

Giacoma, stay in Assisi and help these poor orphan
brothers.

GIACOMA.

Thy wish has ever been my law, and now
This doubly so ; be satisfied, dear friend,
The brothers shall not be uncomforted.

FRANCIS.

Then two women are true to me—thou and Clare.

GIACOMA.

I will tell her thou didst speak of her.

FRANCIS.

Do thou tell her, and say that, dying, I blessed her.
Give her this little cross when I am dead.   [*He sleeps.*

GIACOMA.

Hush !   He will sleep awhile.

ELIAS.

I would he were more reverent of death,
And met it waking with a sinner's fear.

BERNARD.

A saint lies dying there.   Disturb him not.

ELIAS.

[*To the younger* Brothers.] Stand not a-gaping ; get
    ye back a space.

FRANCIS [*In delirium*].

And there shineth the sun divinely manifest,
While azure break the heavens
Above the sombre clouds !
The trees with golden leaves are amorously clothed,
Celestial grow the rocks,
The hillside blooms a single flower,
And peace encamps upon the solemn vales.
And see, the Holy Seraph comes o'er the tree tops
        sailing,
My love to him increasing, as he comes slowly, slowly,
He has the wondrous image of a god crucified,
Upon his head two wings ;
Two covering his body and two outstretched for
        flight,
        He truly bears.—
Ecstatic vision, union mysterious !
On me those wounds are sealed.

ELIAS.

His mind's astray, let him be taken in.

JUNIPER.

Come not near, Elias, at thy peril.

FRANCIS.

Thou givest me calm seas to sail upon,
And peace is on the waters, and the sail
By gale of love is filled to bear us back
To the delightful land of Italy.
Nay, Captain, do not curse the infidel,
Even the dogs eat of the crumbs that fall ;
And I have seen the Holy Sepulchre.

ELIAS.

He must be stayed.

BERNARD.
But these are precious words.

FRANCIS.
I know I shall become a mighty prince ! [*He awakes.*
Is to-day Thursday?

GIACOMA.
Yes.

FRANCIS.
Brother Leo, read to me.

LEO.
What shall I read to thee ?

FRANCIS.
" Ante diem festum Paschae."

LEO [*Reading*].
" Ante diem festum Paschae, sciens Iesus quia
venit hora ejus ut transeat ex hoc mundo ad patrem :
cum dilexisset suos, qui erant in mundo, in finem
dilexit eos.   Et coena facta, cum diabolus iam
misisset in cor ut traderet eum Judas Simonis Is-
cariotae, sciens quia omnia dedit ei Pater in manus,
quia a Deo exiuit, et ad Deum vadit : surgit et ponit
vestimenta sua : et cum accepisset linteum, praecinxit
se.   Deinde mittit aquam in peluim, et cepit lauare
pedes discipulorum "——

FRANCIS.
The sun is almost set ;
Sing, birds and fly,
I soon shall fly and sing with you.
Sister Death,
Mild art thou ;
Come soon.
Sing me the song I made.

BERNARD.

I cannot hear.

FRANCIS.

Sing me my song of praise.

GIACOMA.

" Sing me my song of praise."

BERNARD.

Brothers, let us sing the song of praise.   Come, be brave.

[*The* Brothers *stand up and sing, first in low voice, then with power.*

" Most High, most powerful and gentle Lord,
Thine be praise, glory and power, with all blessing,
And to Thee alone.

Be praised, O Lord, with all Thy works,
And specially for sir brother sun,
Who is Thy day and splendour,
And radiant witness.

Be praised, O Lord, for sister moon and the stars,
In heaven Thou mad'st them wondrous, bright and fair ;
Be praised, O Lord, for brother wind,
And the clouds, and the good and every other weather.

Be praised, O Lord, for our lowly sister water,
So useful, and humble and chaste ;
And for brother fire who lightens darkness,
Who is fair, jocund, robust, and strong.

Be praised, O Lord, for mother earth
Who nourishes us in her government,
Diversely bearing fruit and herb
And many coloured flowers.

Be praised, O Lord, for our Sister Death."

FRANCIS [*Starting up*].
And for our bride Poverty.
> [*He falls back and dies.   The* Brothers *cease
> singing and gather round.   The song
> is continued by unseen spirits.*

" Be praised, O Lord, for those who forgive,
And for love of Thee bear tribulation and pain ;
Blessèd be those who persevere in peace ;
By Thee, O Lord, shall they be crowned."

THE END.

CHISWICK PRESS:—CHARLES WHITTINGHAM AND CO.
TOOKS COURT, CHANCERY LANE, LONDON.

www.ingramcontent.com/pod-product-compliance
Lightning Source LLC
Chambersburg PA
CBHW022013050726
47499CB00007BA/2569